To Phoe

Fairy
Rescuers

Fairy Wishes

Karen Clayton

Fairy Rescuers

Karen Langtree

© Karen Langtree, 2010

Published by OneWay Press

ISBN 978-0-9561086-1-6

Illustrations © Cat O'Neil

Cover design by Cat O'Neil

Prepared and printed by:

York Publishing Services Ltd
64 Hallfield Road
Layerthorpe
York YO31 7ZQ
Tel: 01904 431213

Website: www.yps-publishing.co.uk

Dedication

To my wonderful Ian: Without you I'd still be only dreaming ....

To my lovely children Rachael and Jack: You are always in my heart.

To all at YPS: Thank you for your hard work and integrity.

About the Author

Karen is the author of My Wicked Stepmother. She lives in York with her two children and still has the naughty guinea pigs! As well as being an author she is a primary school teacher and her passion is to see all children enjoying books as much as she does. Her favourite colour is purple and she hates it when you get to the end of a good book and have to say goodbye to the characters!

You can contact Karen via her website www.karenlangtree.com or email her at karen.langtree@btinternet.com

Karen loves to hear from her readers and replies to every email.

About the Illustrator

Cat O'Neil is an Edinburgh based student illustrator, originally from York. She loves to draw and has a very impressive collection of pens. She is currently a student at Edinburgh College of Art, and hopes to eventually work as a freelance illustrator for newspapers and magazines. Her main focus is medical and scientific editorials, however she also likes to do experimental and exciting side projects and collaborations. These include animations, book illustrations and comics about her three cats (including moon-cat, who likes to go deep sea diving).

You can contact Cat via her website www.catoneil.co.uk

Chapter One

The Thing

'Ugh, what's this?' shouted Callum, pulling out a manky looking thing from underneath a pile of wood.

Five year old Callum was looking for insects, as he always did when let loose in the garden. He was putting them into an ice-cream tub. He already had two snails, a large black beetle and three worms. The thing he was holding was not an insect. Callum held it up to eye level, by what appeared to be a leg. It hung limply.

'It's dead,' he said.

Ellie climbed down from the tree she was sitting in and came over. 'Let me see,' she said, making a grab for the thing.

'Get off, it's mine!' Callum swung the thing away from Ellie and ran round to the back of the shed.

She followed. 'Go on Cal, give me a look. I might be able to tell you what it is.'

'Only look, don't touch,' he said, dangling the thing in front of Ellie's eyes.

It was about ten centimetres long and very grubby. But underneath the dirt there was a bluey-green shimmer. Ellie turned her head upside down. It appeared to have a tiny face, with closed eyes and a green head. Two long wings were bedraggled and damaged.

'It could be some sort of dragonfly,' Ellie suggested. 'It would be a very big one though. Anyway, it definitely looks dead.' She reached out a finger to prod it.

'Hands off!' ordered Callum, swinging the thing away.

'Do you really want it if it's dead already? I thought you liked to kill them yourself.'

Callum gave this some thought. 'I want it.'

'Well put it in another box, or the other creepy crawlies might eat it. I'll go and get one.' Ellie ran to the house to find a container. She came back with a margarine tub. 'I can't find the lid, but stick it in there for now.'

Callum dumped the thing in the tub and left it by the woodpile. Then he was off to look for more insects. When she saw that he was engrossed in the old vegetable patch beyond the tree, Ellie picked up the tub. She studied the little dead creature. She had never seen anything like it and didn't really think it was a dragonfly. She touched it. It was soft. Suddenly, it twitched. Ellie pulled her finger back. The thing made a noise that sounded like a tiny groan. Then it was silent. She touched it again. This time it didn't move. She gently stroked her finger over its body, which seemed to have human looking arms and legs. Surely she must be mistaken, but it appeared to be wearing clothes. They were torn. What she had thought was a green head, was actually a little cap; Ellie could see wisps of brown hair falling from it. The most disturbing thing for Ellie was that the thing had a very human looking face.

It could be an old toy, but she was sure it had moved and groaned. In her mind an idea was forming which she was trying to avoid. It couldn't be. There were no such things. But the idea was so strong that it burst out of her lips in a whisper.

'Could this be a fairy?'

She had to make sure it was a living (if only just) creature. She scooped it out of the tub, checking to see that Callum was still busy down the garden. He was. She turned it carefully in her hands, trying to think of what her mum would do if Ellie was hurt. She would probably put her to bed and make her drink a lot. That's what Ellie would do with this thing. She would have to hide it from Callum so that she had time to see if her experiment worked.

She put the empty tub back by the woodpile and carried the thing up to her bedroom. Laying it on her bed, she scrabbled around in the mess to find something suitable. She found a shoebox, which had long ago been a bed for one of her dolls.

She placed the thing into the bed, trying to prop it up against the pillow. It slumped to one side. Ellie then went to the bathroom with a little doll's goblet. She tried to fill it with water but it was so small, and the

4

water gushed so fast that it was impossible to fill. She went back to the bedroom to look for something better. Under her bed she found the lid from an old plastic bottle. She washed it out and filled it with water.

How was she going to get the thing to drink? Its mouth was so tiny. The bottle top was as big as a washing up bowl would be to a human. In the end she decided she would just have to try it. Lifting the thing out of the bed, she tilted the bottle lid in the direction of its mouth. The contents splashed over the whole face and the thing shuddered and coughed. Its eyes opened wide and its arms and legs twitched several times. Then it lay, lifelessly, in Ellie's hand again. Ellie was startled. It had been alive. Had she drowned it?

She shook it. 'Wake up thing!'

But it didn't. As Ellie dried it, her eyes began to sting and everything went blurry. She swiped at them with the towel. Panic began to churn her insides. Should she call her mum? No, it was too weird. No one knew about it. She put the thing back in the little bed, tucking it in for good measure. Then she hid it under her bed. Perhaps it had just gone back to sleep she told herself.

But in her heart, she was sure she had killed it.

'Mummy, Ellie stole my thing!' shouted Callum from downstairs. Mum was on the computer in the dining room. 'Mummy!'

'What, Callum! I'm trying to write a lesson plan.'

Mum was a primary school teacher. She spent a lot of time on the computer. She came out into the hall.

'Ellie has stolen my special thing I found in the garden,' Callum whined.

'Stolen, you mean. What special thing?'

'I found it: a special big bug, with wings and legs like a person.'

'Wings and legs like a person? I'm sure Ellie didn't steal it. Where did you put it?'

'It was in here,' he said, showing her the empty margarine tub.

Mum called up the stairs. 'Ellie, come down a minute please.' Ellie appeared, jumping down the stairs as innocently as possible. 'What's all this about?' asked Mum.

'Oh it's that stupid thing he found...'

'It's not stupid. It was special and you stealed it!'

'Stole, Callum, stole. Well, did you Ellie?' asked Mum.

'It must have escaped. He left it by the woodpile and the tub didn't have a lid on. It was quite big so it could easily have got out. And it had wings.'

'But it was dead,' said Callum.

Ellie flushed. *It is now*, she thought.

'It wasn't dead. It moved a bit. It was just stunned. It probably recovered when you were down the garden, and got away.'

Callum began to cry. 'It didn't. You steal... stoled it.'

Mum looked at Ellie, who shrugged. 'Now then, Callum,' Mum said. 'Haven't you got lots of other insects? Come and show me what else you've collected.' Mum guided Callum back into the garden to find his ice-cream tub.

Ellie ran upstairs and threw herself on her bed. She felt even more rotten now. She had killed a strange creature *and* lied to her Mum.

Chapter Two

Lucy

It was a beautiful spring morning: sunny and not too cold. It was Monday and time for school. That meant lots of shouting, grumping and frantic searching for things. Ellie liked school and today she was double glad to be going. She couldn't wait to get away from her bedroom and the thought of the dead creature under her bed. Of course she would have to get rid of it after school, but at least she had a few hours with her friends to forget about it.

She was first at the door, eight o'clock on the dot.

'Wow, this must be a miracle!' exclaimed Mum. 'Something good happening today?'

'I hope so,' muttered Ellie. Mum gave her a quizzical look then shouted up the stairs. 'Callum, hurry up! We need to go.'

Callum and Ellie had to go to breakfast club every morning because Mum had to be at her school by 8:30. Their dad was a doctor, so he was rarely able to take them to school. He was usually working or sleeping.

At school Ellie met up with her other friends, who went to breakfast club: Tom and Rhys. They were swapping the latest game cards. 'Hey guys,' she said, unenthusiastically.

'What's up El? You had a bad weekend?'

'Nah, was ok. What about you?'

'Went skateboarding,' said Tom. 'Me and my dad. He's rubbish but it makes me look even better.'

'I went to my nan's. Boring. But she does make great chocolate cake,' Rhys said.

'You should come skateboarding El. You're good at it. Not as good as me of course. Dad wouldn't mind. You could come too Rhys.'

'So why does your face look like someone trod on it then, El?' asked Rhys.

'Oh it's nothing really. Don't want to talk about it.'

Ellie sloped away to play on the computers. She so wanted to forget about the creature under her bed, but it was there in her mind, grabbing at every thought. *Fairy, fairy. You killed a fairy!* It was like a manic song going round and round her head. In class she usually worked hard, but today Mrs. Leeson thought she must have had a late night and was threatening to speak to her mum. By lunchtime Ellie wanted to scream.

Tom and Rhys were playing football with some others, so she joined in. Not many girls were allowed to play, but Ellie was a great keeper, so she was always popular. She wasn't afraid to dive for the ball and often won the game for her side by her excellent goal keeping.

9

She played for the town under elevens. Today her team lost. She let two goals in.

'Can't believe you let two in El. What the matter with you?' Peter Tyler said, as the game finished.

'Everyone has an off day,' said Tom, coming to his friend's defence. 'Give her a break.'

'She played worse than a girl,' Peter shouted, running off. Tom was about to run after him.

'Aw forget him,' Ellie said, shrugging, 'He's not worth it. And he's right anyway.'

She headed to the loo. While she was in the cubicle she heard a group of girls come in. It sounded like they all crammed into one cubicle. There was some banging and then Ellie heard crying.

'I never snitched on you,' sobbed the crying girl. 'I wouldn't, cos I know you'd do this.'

'Shut up, you cry baby. We're gonna teach you a lesson.'

Ellie recognised the voice. It was Nikki Walters from year six. She and her little gang had a reputation for picking on younger girls. Nikki had already been excluded once, but that didn't stop her.

The other girls sniggered and one said, 'Yeah, blubby pants. You'd better think of a good story about how you got those bruises, or they'll be worse next time.'

'What... bruises?' the girl asked, foolishly, between sobs.

'These ones, stupid,' Nikki snarled. Just as she said that, sharp nails from under the cubicle wall, dug into her ankle. She yelped and tried to kick them off but they held on. Ellie was glad she had finally listened to her mum about not biting her nails.

'You little... Who are you? Wait 'til I get hold of you.'

The bullies, all four of them, forgot their victim for a moment and pushed out of the cubicle. Ellie was waiting. She could see past them to a frightened year three girl, sitting on the loo seat lid. She didn't really know the girl.

'Leave her alone,' Ellie said, folding her arms.

'You gonna make us?' said Nikki, taking a step towards Ellie. The four girls moved in behind Nikki.

Ellie didn't move. She tried to speak firmly and not let her racing heart give her away.

'If you push it, yeah,' said Ellie.

The girls sniggered. 'Don't you know who you're talking to?' said Nikki, breathing down into Ellie's face.

Ellie tried not to flinch. 'Yes. Everyone knows who you are. But I bet you don't know who *you're* messing with?'

Nikki, smiled, almost admiring Ellie's nerve. 'Go on then, tell us.'

'I'm Ellie Deaver, best under eleven goalie in town, and karate expert, and if you make me, I'll put you on the floor, then I'll do the same to your gormless girly gang!'

Ellie thought she saw a flicker of worry pass over their faces. Nikki hesitated, but couldn't risk looking cowardly. 'What a load of rubbish. Like to see you try, karate kid!' She raised her fist to thump Ellie.

The others laughed, but not for long, because in an instant Nikki Walters was lying on her back on the toilet floor. The others looked astonished. Ellie smiled. 'Next.'

'Help me up you lot,' Nikki groaned.

The girls helped Nikki to her feet. She was fighting back tears. 'Just you wait Ellie Deaver!'

Ellie pushed past her, grabbed the year three girl's hand and walked, as calmly as she could, out of the toilets.

Outside, the girl looked at Ellie in admiration. 'Thanks, Ellie Deaver.'

'You're welcome,' said Ellie, leaning against a wall with her eyes shut. She was shaking.

'I thought you were kidding them about the karate thing.'

'Nah. I go to lessons. It's really good. I've never used it outside class before. It's all about self-control you see. Not really supposed to do that, but if you're in a tight corner you know you can get out of it.'

'You didn't have to save me,' the girl said, shyly. 'You could have just sneaked out.'

'What? Knowing they were bullying someone again. Not my style.'

'Well. Thanks anyway.'

'What's your name?'

'Lucy.'

'You should come to karate, Lucy, then you'd have confidence to stick up to people like that.'

'I couldn't. My mum wouldn't let me. She would think it's too boyish. She only lets me do ballet and brownies.'

'Well, if she knew what was happening with those bullies she'd let you. Tell her about them.'

'Oh... I will. Thanks Ellie. I'd better go now.'

'See you, Lucy.'

By the end of the day, Ellie was famous. Several year sixes stopped her on the way out of school to ask if she had really floored Nikki Walters. Ellie just shrugged and wished they'd go away. She didn't like being the centre of attention.

Chapter Three

The Creature

When she got home Ellie rushed upstairs to look under her bed.

'Hi Ellie,' her gran shouted. 'You're in a hurry. Are you all right?'

'Yes Gran, just looking for something.'

She knelt by the bed and hesitated. She had decided firmly that the creature was not a fairy. Her imagination had been playing tricks on her. She was going to bury the creature down the garden. But now the time had come, she felt sick. Facing up to Nikki Walters was nothing compared to this.

She took a deep breath and stretched her arm under the bed to find the box. She pulled it out; her eyes closed tight. With the box by her knee, she opened one eye and then the other.

Two small green eyes peered up at her. 'Hello,' said a faint, hoarse voice. 'More water please.'

Shocked, Ellie ran to the bathroom to fill the bottle lid again. 'How should I … how are you going to drink it?' she stammered.

The creature reached out her hands. Ellie passed her the lid. She took it and lapped the water from it like a dog would do. She was so weak that she almost dropped it, but Ellie held it in place. When she had finished drinking, the creature lay back against the doll's pillow, exhausted.

'Thank-you,' she said, closing her eyes.

'Wait, don't go,' said Ellie, as if the creature might be about to die all over again. 'Who... I mean, what are you?'

The creature did not stir. However, Ellie was relieved to see its tiny chest move up and down, breathing softly. She gently tucked it in and sat on the floor staring at it. Here, in the bedroom of Ellie Deaver (best under eleven goalie in town – most famous karate kid in the school) lay a real live fairy. She didn't know what to do with it. She couldn't exactly tell anyone, or call for a fairy doctor! But she didn't want it to die. She would have to read up on fairies and in the meantime just keep it warm, give it water and feed it. But what would she feed it? This was the first thing to find out.

'I'm just going on the computer Gran,' said Ellie from the dining room.

'Well you are a busy bee this evening. No time for a cuddle with your old gran even?' Gran said, smiling round the door.

Ellie hugged her. ' 'Course.'

'You up to something for school then?'

'No, just something I want to find out.'

'Ah well, the Internet is a good place to look then, so I hear.'

When Gran had gone back to the lounge Ellie typed FAIRY into Google. A massive list of websites faced her. Fairy stories, fairy toys, Fairy cleaning agents, Fairy facts. *How can there be fairy facts*, she thought, *when fairies don't even* ...She looked up fairy facts.

It was a web site dedicated to all the folklore and traditions surrounding fairies. There she found that fairies were said to eat nuts, pine kernels and berries, bread and even chocolate!

'What you doing?' said Callum, at her shoulder.

She hadn't realised he was there. 'Just looking at something,' Ellie replied.

'F-a-i-r-y,' he spelt out, 'fairy. Why are you looking about fairies? You don't believe in fairies.'

'I know, Callum. Go away.'

'No,' said Callum. 'I want to look about fairies.'

'No you don't,' Ellie replied. 'Boys don't bother about fairies. Go away. Stop pestering me.' She gave him a shove.

'Gran,' he wailed, 'Ellie pushed me!'

Gran came into the room. Ellie quickly exited the site.

'What's going on here?'

'Nothing Gran. He's pestering me.'

'Come on Callum, leave Ellie to her research.'

'No I want to see. She's got my thing that's a fairy and I want it back.'

'What are you talking about Cal?' Ellie laughed, nervously. 'There's no such thing as fairies.'

'Why are you looking about them on the computer then?'

'What are you looking up Ellie?' asked Gran.

Ellie glared at Callum. 'I am looking up things about fairies Gran. It's… for someone at school.' Ellie felt herself going red. She didn't like telling lies.

'Well, come on Callum. Leave your sister alone.' Gran took Callum by the hand and led him, protesting, out of the room.

Ellie went to the kitchen to find bread. She made sure the coast was clear and tiptoed up to her room. The thing … fairy was still sleeping. Where could she keep it? It didn't feel right to shove it under the bed, with all her junk, now it was alive, but she had to keep it hidden. She put the sleeping fairy in her horse's stable. Light was able to get in through the door. She placed the bread on a piece of tissue beside the bed, with some more water.

'Wake up soon, fairy. Please,' she whispered.

The next day at school Ellie was still worried about the fairy. She had been pleased to see this morning though that some of the bread had been eaten and some of the water had been drunk. At least the fairy was still alive. Ellie wanted to talk to it, to find out where it was from and what had happened to it. She was quite excited really, despite her former unbelief in such girly things.

At lunchtime she was playing football with Tom, Rhys and the others. She dreaded to think what would happen if they found out she believed in fairies. Out of the corner of her eye she noticed a girl waving at her from the sideline. It was Lucy, the girl she had rescued yesterday. After the match (which her team won 2-1) she went to say hi.

'Hi,' Lucy said. 'You really are a good goalie.'

'Thanks,' said Ellie. 'I love football.'

'Don't you get hurt by the ball?' asked Lucy.

Ellie smiled. 'Yeah, sometimes, but I don't really notice it. I just want to keep it out of the net. The goalie is really important to the team.'

'Yes, I know,' said Lucy. 'They're lucky to have you.'

Ellie blushed. 'Thanks. Anyway, are you ok today? Did you tell your mum about those girls?'

Lucy looked down at her feet.

'You didn't? Why not? Don't you want to stop them?'

'They told me that if I told anyone they'd been picking on me and stealing things from other kids too, I'd be for it. That's why they had me in the toilets.'

'Well, you should tell on them. Haven't you even told your teacher?'

Lucy shook her head.

'Well you should. I'll look out for you Lucy, but I can't always be there and that Nikki Walters knows that. She'll never stop bullying if she keeps getting away with it.'

'I know. And she's after you now too.'

'I can look after myself,' said Ellie.

Lucy grinned. 'I know. You were amazing.'

'I tell you what? Why don't I talk to your mum about Karate on the way out of school this afternoon? Then we could tell her why together.'

Lucy bit her lip. 'Well…ok.'

'I'll meet you by the Year Three door then.'

The whistle went and the girls walked towards their lines to go into school.

'By the way Lucy,' Ellie began, 'do you know anything about…' she looked around her, then whispered, 'fairies?'

Lucy looked at Ellie in surprise. 'I didn't think you would believe in fairies.'

'Shh,' Ellie hissed. 'Well, I'm not saying I do, but are you interested in them?'

'Oh yes, I love fairies…'

'Shh, keep your voice down,' Ellie said, just resisting putting her hand over Lucy's mouth.

Lucy giggled and whispered,' Yes, I've got lots of fairy books and some dolls and a fairy make over kit and…'

'Ok, ok I get it,' said Ellie.

'Why?' asked Lucy.

'Never mind, got to go. See you later.'

Mrs. Pennington frowned and pulled all sorts of disapproving faces as Ellie and Lucy told her about the bullies and the Karate.

'Well,' she said in her rather posh voice, 'Thank you for looking after Lucy, Ellie. I will have to talk to the Head about this girl. He needs to do something about her.'

'And what about Karate?' Ellie asked.

'Oh no, Lucy can't so something like that. She wouldn't like getting hurt and it's not very lady-like is it?'

Lucy scowled. 'But Mummy....'

'Lucy darling, I have your best interests at heart.'

Lucy looked down at her feet and sighed. Ellie didn't give up so easily.

'Shotokan Karate, which is what I do, is all about self-control, self-confidence and respect. It is about avoiding violence where possible and being very disciplined.'

Mrs. Pennington was starting to look impressed so Ellie continued. 'It's a very ancient Japanese art and requires a lot of skill and concentration. They say it improves your performance at school all round.' She was really glad her Karate instructor kept drumming all this stuff into them.

Mrs. Pennington pursed her lips and gave Ellie a sort of smile. 'Well, thank you very much for the information, Ellie. I'll ... think about it. Come along Lucy.'

Mrs. Pennington turned and walked away.

'It's six o'clock Thursday at the Dunston Road Sports Centre,' Ellie offered.

'Bye,' Lucy said.

'See you,' Ellie replied.

'Oh, I'll see what I can find out about you-know-whats for you,' shouted Lucy, as she disappeared round the corner.

Ellie waved nervously. She shouldn't have mentioned fairies to Lucy.

Chapter Four

Gabriella

Ellie jogged home. She was eager to look at her fairy. 'Hi Gran,' she shouted, dumping her bag in the kitchen and grabbing an apple.

'Hi love,' called Gran coming to greet her. 'Had a nice day?'

'Yes thanks.'

'Do you want a drink? Callum is watching Ceebeebies.'

'I'm ok thanks Gran. Think I'll go and play upstairs.'

'Ok love,' said Gran, heading back to snuggle up on the sofa with Callum.

Ellie shut her bedroom door and bent down to peer inside the stable.

To her delight, the fairy was awake and sitting up in the bed. She smiled at Ellie. 'Hello,' she said, still a little weakly.

'Hi,' said Ellie. 'I'm glad you're awake. I was really worried about you.'

'I think you saved my life,' said the fairy.

Ellie blushed. 'Well, I wouldn't go that far, but you have been really poorly. Have you tried to get up or…fly.'

'Yes,' said the fairy. 'I can walk, and I don't think any bones are broken, but I can't fly. Look at my wing.'

'I know. Will it mend like skin does?'

'No, it will have to be repaired.'

'Oh. Can I help with that?'

'I'm not sure,' said the fairy, 'and all my magical powers seem to have disappeared.'

'Oh dear,' said Ellie, wondering what it must be like to have magical powers. 'I probably can't help with that either.' There was a pause. 'What's your name?'

'I don't know,' the fairy replied, her face crumpling. 'I don't know who I am, where I am or how I got here in this state.'

'Gosh, that's awful. And I don't know much about fairies. I never even believed in them 'til I found you.'

The fairy looked shocked.

'I do now of course,' Ellie added quickly. 'My name's Ellie by the way. Maybe we could give you a name until you remember your own.'

'That would be nice. What have you got in mind?'

Ellie looked around her room. On her walls were posters of her favourite football team and some pop stars. 'How about Gabriella?' she suggested.

'That sounds beautiful,' said the fairy.

'Do you want some more food? I didn't know what to bring you. Would you like some of my apple?'

'Yes please. The bread is nice too, thank you.'

Ellie bit into her apple and broke some off for Gabriella. They ate, silently, for a while.

'So don't you know anything about yourself?' Ellie asked.

'All I can remember is a horrible ugly goblin face looming over me; then his voice screeching 'Die!' After that, there was a bright flash of light and I was falling. The next thing I remember is you.'

'Wow, that must have been scary. Don't you remember where you're from or any of your family and friends?'

'I know I'm a fairy, so I must be from Fairyland. But I can't remember anyone else or how to get back there.' Gabriella looked as if she was about to cry.

'Well, somehow we'll find out,' said Ellie. 'And we have to find out who wanted you dead because he sounds dangerous to me.'

Ellie felt like a detective but she had no clues at this moment as to how to solve this mystery. 'Can I clean your clothes for you? You could wear some of my dolls clothes while I do it.'

'Thank you,' said Gabriella. 'May I bathe as well?'

'Erm…yes, but I'll have to think of somewhere small enough.'

'Fairies only bathe in rainwater,' Gabriella said. 'Otherwise their wings get damaged.' She looked at her broken one and sighed.

'We have a water butt down the garden to collect rainwater. You could have a shower under the tap. And I'll bring a clean face cloth that you could use as a towel. We'll have to be careful though because I don't want the others to see you. My brother would want to … well, never mind about that. Are you strong enough to do it now?'

'Yes please,' said Gabriella.

Ellie lifted her gently and put her into her shirt pocket. She fetched the face cloth and gathered together some dolls clothes. 'Are you ok in there?' she whispered.

'Yes, I'm fine,' came the reply.

Ellie sneaked downstairs and out into the garden. The water butt was hidden from view of the house so it was easy for Gabriella to have her shower in private. Ellie turned the tap from the water butt so that a slow trickle came out. 'Don't you mind it being cold?'

'No, it's perfect,' said Gabriella.

Afterwards she put on the dolls jeans and cropped top Ellie had brought for her. The top opened at the back so that Gabriella's wings could come out. Ellie watched as the fairy combed through her soft fine hair with her fingers. Then Ellie washed Gabriella's own clothes in the rainwater. The mud came off instantly and they sparkled at once in the sunlight.

'Thanks for that, I feel much better now.'

Ellie took Gabriella back to her room. 'I'll have to do more research into fairies,' she said. 'Then maybe I can find out how to get you back to Fairyland.'

'It's strange,' said Gabriella, 'People who don't believe in fairies can't normally see them.' She looked thoughtfully at Ellie. 'You must have a special job to do.'

'Well maybe it's to help you find your way home. First we should try to repair your wing. Can I sew it back together with a needle and thread?' asked Ellie, worrying about the fact that she had never sewn anything in her life.

Gabriella thought about a human sized needle and shook her head. 'I think I remember something about spiders helping with fairy repairs. Do you know any spiders?'

Ellie thought this was funny. 'Well I don't have any spider friends,' she giggled, 'but I'm sure we have spiders that come out of cracks and corners in the house. And there will be a few cobwebs, I think. Mum's not hot on dusting.'

'I'll look round your house to find one. You all seem to go out during the day.'

'We go to school and my Mum and Dad are at work. Just be careful of my brother Callum. He's the one that found you first and, let's put it this way, he's not very gentle. I'd better go downstairs now. My mum will be home soon and Gran will be wondering what I'm doing. I'll see you later.'

'Ok Ellie. Thanks.'

Later that night, when Ellie came back up to bed, she found Gabriella fast asleep in her little bed, in the stable. Ellie smiled and climbed into her own bed. She couldn't quite believe she had a real live fairy in her room. Tomorrow she would try to work out how to get Gabriella back to Fairyland.

During the night, Gabriella was woken by a shaft of moonlight that had managed to sneak its way through the stable door. As she lay in the beam of light something like a warm liquid began filling her up, starting at her feet. At first it felt strange, but then it felt lovely. By the time it had reached her head she felt wonderful. She leapt out of bed and began dancing across Ellie's floor. She looked up at the moon, who smiled back at her, and she realised his beams had made her better.

'Thank you Moon,' she whispered, blowing him a kiss. 'Now I must look for a spider to mend my wing.'

She looked around the room. It was difficult to see any cobwebs on the ceiling because it was so far away and she couldn't fly up to it. She looked in corners for cracks and soon she found one. She peered in but it was too dark to see anything and she was too big to climb inside. She called into it.

'Is anyone there? Mrs. Spider can you hear me?'

She waited and waited. She was just about to give up, when a spider with long legs appeared.

'Oh,' the spider exclaimed. 'I've never seen a fairy here before. Can I help you my dear?'

'Yes please, if you would be so kind. I have a damaged wing and was wondering if you would mend it for me.'

Gabriella showed her the wing.

'I am honoured to do anything I can to help a fairy. Turn around, I'll have it mended in no time.'

Gabriella turned and sat down. The spider began sewing the wing back together. Her silver thread blended beautifully with the silver strands in Gabriella's wings. The pattern was very intricate and the spider matched it perfectly.

'There you are my dear.'

Gabriella stood up and began to flutter her wings. She lifted off the ground and hovered for some seconds.

'Oh thank you, thank you Mrs. Spider!'

'You are most welcome little fairy. Take care now,' and off she scuttled back to her home.

Gabriella was so happy that she picked up one of Ellie's Action Men and began to dance with him. He was stiff and difficult to move with.

'If only he was alive,' she thought. Then she decided to try something. She shook her fingers over his head and at once a host of fairy dust scattered over him. He opened his eyes. Gabriella squealed in delight.

' My magic is back!' She wanted to wake Ellie and tell her, forgetting she had just brought the Action Man to life.

'Excuse me beautiful lady but may I have this dance?' asked the man.

'Oh,' she giggled, 'I'd love to.'

And although the music was only in her head, Gabriella danced round the room, with the Action Man, trying not to bump into Ellie's toys scattered across the floor.

When they had finished she thanked him for the dance and turned him back into a toy. Then she flopped into her bed and fell into an exhausted but happy sleep.

Chapter Five

Becoming Friends

When Ellie awoke, Gabriella was fast asleep, so Ellie tried not to disturb her. At school she asked if she could have a special pass to use the computers at lunchtime. It was very unusual for Ellie not to be playing football outside, however, she needed to look on the Internet to see if she could find out how to get to Fairyland. She still couldn't quite believe she was doing this. And she certainly didn't want any of her friends to find out. After a whole lunchtime of searching, she was none the wiser and to make matters worse, some boys from her football team had seen her and were sniggering at her for looking at fairy things. Just Great!

She was in a very bad mood when Lucy ran up to her after school.

'Hi Ellie,' she said. 'I've got something for you, but my mum won't let me bring it to school.' She looked around, then lowered her voice. 'It's called the Encyclopedia of Fairytopia. It's really big. It might help.'

'Thanks Lucy,' said Ellie. 'I've been on the Internet at lunchtime but got nowhere. How can I get it?'

Well,' Lucy began, 'I was wondering if I might come round to your house at the weekend.'

Ellie hesitated. If Lucy came she would certainly find out about Gabriella. Would that be wise? But, on the other hand Lucy could be useful, with her fairy knowledge. 'Ok. Ask your mum. It will be ok with mine. Saturday morning: About ten. And hide the book. I don't want anyone knowing about me and ... fairies.'

'Of course,' Lucy said, grinning.

When Ellie arrived back in her bedroom she found Gabriella sitting on top of her bookshelf. She had changed back into her fairy clothes, which shimmered bluey green in the sunlight.

'How did you...'

Gabriella lifted off, fluttering her wings and showering Ellie with colourful dust which made her giggle and sneeze at the same time.

'Wow, your wings are mended. But how?'

Gabriella told Ellie about the spider and the moon. She didn't tell her about the Action Man, as she felt rather embarrassed about it.

'I read on the Internet today about the moon being special to fairies. And to have your powers back is great. Can you remember who you are now?'

Gabriella sat down on Ellie's pillow. Ellie carefully sat on the duvet.

'I can remember more about being a fairy, but not about *who* I am. And I still don't know how to get back. But I have a much stronger sense that I must. Something bad is happening in Fairyland. You are going to help me do something about it Ellie. I feel that strongly too.'

'Gabriella,' Ellie began, 'I have a friend. Her name is Lucy and she knows a lot more than I do about fairy things. Would you meet her? I think she can help us.'

'Yes, of course I will. If she's a friend of fairies and she could help, then I must meet her.'

On Saturday morning Lucy arrived, clutching a large book in a plastic bag.

'Ellie, your friend is here,' shouted Dad up the stairs.

'Ellie came bounding down. 'Hi Lucy, come on in.'

'I'll pick you up later Lucy. What time?' Lucy's dad looked at Ellie's dad.

'Can she stay for tea Dad? Please?' Ellie asked.

'Fine by me,' her dad said. 'Pick her up about five?'

Mr. Pennington nodded and Ellie and Lucy hurried upstairs. Ellie stopped at her bedroom door.

'Now before we go in Lucy,' she said, getting serious, 'You have to promise me that you will keep all this a secret.'

'I will. I know you've got your image to keep up,' Lucy said, trying to wink at Ellie.

'Yes, but I'm going to show you something, and you'll probably want to tell your friends about it.'

'I won't Ellie. I promise: Brownie's honour.'

Ellie gave Lucy one more serious look then smiled. 'Ok, I believe you.'

As Lucy walked in to Ellie's room she was amazed at the mess. 'Wow, my mum would go mad at this. She makes me tidy my toys away every night.'

Ellie shrugged. 'Mum's too busy to worry about messy bedrooms.'

'Do you see anything ...different?' asked Ellie, mysteriously.

Lucy scanned the room. All of a sudden a little green thing flew out of the stable and landed on the desk. Then it lifted up again, flying right up to Ellie and perched on her shoulder. This time Lucy saw a trail of colourful dust floating behind it as it flew.

She squealed in delight. 'Oh a real live fairy!'

'Keep your voice down,' said Ellie, laughing. 'The last thing we want is Callum in here. He's already suspicious that I've got something special. He's tried hunting for Gabriella but she's managed to hide from him.'

'Oh is that your name?' asked Lucy, talking to the fairy now. 'I'm so excited to meet you. It's like a dream come true.'

Lucy was bubbling over. Gabriella and Ellie told her the whole story. Lucy got her book out. 'I know there are things in this book about magical places for getting into Fairyland.'

The three of them studied the book for ages.

'Look,' said Lucy. 'It says here that there are fairy paths down which fairies come into the human world and get back to Fairyland. Where did you say you found Gabriella?'

'By the woodpile next to the shed,' said Ellie.

'Maybe that's a magical path. We should go and look,' Lucy said.

'I'm not going back on my own,' said Gabriella. 'What if that horrible goblin is waiting for me? I'm sure Ellie is meant to come with me.'

'But how?' asked Ellie. 'I'm not magic and I'd be a giant in your land.'

'Maybe my magic is powerful enough to bring you with me and shrink you.'

'Worth a try,' said Ellie.

'What about me?' asked Lucy, looking a bit disappointed.

Gabriella and Ellie looked at her. 'She will probably be useful,' said Ellie. 'She's clever and look how she's helped already.'

'I would be helpful, really. Please let me come.'

'What about the goblins? It's going to be dangerous Lucy,' Gabriella pointed out.

Lucy bit her lip. 'I know. I'll try to be brave.' She looked at Ellie, who smiled back at her.

Thinking about the danger, Ellie quickly gathered together some things that might be useful. She knew her dad had a penknife that he used when they went camping. She found it and put it in her pocket.

'Come on, let's go and investigate the path,' said Ellie.

Gabriella flew into Ellie's pocket and lay still. The girls sneaked downstairs and into the garden. They scouted around the woodpile, behind the shed and even in the shed.

'How will we know where the path is?' asked Ellie.

Gabriella flittered about their heads. 'I wish I could remember. I should be able to tell.'

'Stand exactly where Ellie found you, Gabriella,' said Lucy. 'And see if you feel anything.'

Gabriella came to rest on the spot where Callum, to be precise, had picked her up.

'Do you feel anything?' asked Lucy.

'Yes, I feel strange. I feel tingly, like when the moon made me well. But this time it's… it's pulling on me.' Gabriella flew up into the air, away from the spot. 'I think this is it. I think I will be pulled back to Fairyland if I stand there much longer. We need to try some magic on you two to see if you can come with me. Let's stand together. I'll sprinkle you with fairy dust, then if you shrink, hold hands with me and we'll see if the force will pull us all back to Fairyland.'

The girls stood as close to the woodpile as possible. Gabriella flew over them and was just about to shower them with dust when a voice called out, 'Ellie, what are you doing? Are you looking for more creatures?'

It was Callum. Quickly, Gabriella flew behind the shed.

'No Cal, we were just… playing hide and seek.'

'Can I play?' he asked.

'No,' said Ellie. 'It's just me and Lucy.'

'Oh. I want to play.'

'Go away, Cal.'

'No!' He folded his arms and scowled at Ellie.

'I think he should play,' said Lucy. 'Its more fun with three.'

Ellie looked at her as if she was mad. Lucy gave her a *trust me* look.

Ellie shrugged. 'Ok Cal, you can play.'

'Right Ellie you're the counter. Give us fifty then come and find us. Ok Callum, come on.'

Lucy looked around for a place to get Callum out of sight. The best place was actually the shed. 'Quick, Callum,' she whispered, 'in here. She'll never think you'd stayed so close.' Callum ran inside, giggling loudly.

Lucy ran round the back and beckoned to Gabriella. They met up with Ellie. 'Keep counting,' whispered Lucy.

'Twenty five, twenty six,' continued Ellie.

'Do it now, Gabriella,' Lucy said.

They all stood on the spot. Gabriella sprinkled the dust. 'Thirty seven, thirty eight ...' The girls felt strange, like you feel when you sit in the bath and the water is draining away. They were being pulled down. Everything was getting taller. The woodpile became a mountain, the trees became giants and the grass became a jungle.

Gabriella stood beside them, looking like she might faint. 'Hold my hand, quickly,' she said, 'it's pulling me.'

Then the girls felt it too. They held Gabriella's hand tightly. There was a whooshing noise. 'I'm scared,' shouted Lucy above the wind.

'Me too,' said Ellie.

Suddenly a gust of wind picked them up and they were being blown like leaves along a path of golden light, which they could now see emerging ahead of them. At first they tumbled over and over, but then Gabriella realised that if she flew with the wind, it steadied them all. *If only the girls could have wings*, she thought.

Chapter Six

Arrival

It was not a smooth flight to Fairyland and a rather bumpy landing. They found themselves in a wood, fortunately having come down *by* the stream and not *in* it!

'That was… different,' said Ellie, rubbing her leg.

'Are you both ok?' asked Gabriella. 'I'm so sorry. I'm sure it's not meant to be like that. I think you not having wings made it difficult. I thought my magic might have given you wings but maybe only real fairies can have them.'

Lucy had bumped her head as she came down and was trying very hard not to cry.

'You ok, Lucy?' asked Ellie. 'Maybe you should have stayed behind.'

'I'll be all right. Anyway, you need me, like Gabriella needs you.'

Ellie laughed. 'I think you're right. You sorted Callum for us. Maybe we need each other.'

Gabriella tried to get up but she couldn't. 'I think there's still something wrong with me. Every time I do some magic, I feel worn out.'

'We should rest for a while then,' said Lucy. 'And maybe you should try not to use your magic unless you really need to.'

The two girls and the fairy sat facing each other. Ellie put her hand out, palm down. Lucy put hers on top. Gabriella followed the pattern. Then they each put their other hand into the pile. 'Together, whatever!' said Ellie.

'Together, whatever!' they all chorused.

As they rested, talking and laughing, Ellie noticed a figure slip behind one of the trees.

'Come on,' she said to the others, 'let's get out of here. You never know who's lurking about, especially if this is the place where the goblin sent Gabriella flying into our world.'

'That's true,' said Gabriella, looking around, warily. The figure had now disappeared and Ellie didn't want to frighten the others, so she didn't say anything about it.

'Do you know where we're heading Gabriella?' asked Lucy.

'I'm afraid not,' said the fairy, 'let's just try to find our way out of these woods. They're actually giving me the creeps.'

It was becoming much darker and colder. The girls walked and Gabriella flew, trying to pick out a path. They looked for a clearing but it seemed a very long way.

'This seems a very strange place for a path into Fairyland to lead,' said Lucy. 'I'd imagined Fairyland to be a beautiful place.'

'From what I remember, it is, Lucy,' said Gabriella, 'but something strange is going on.'

Ellie walked at the back, now and again turning suddenly to see if they were being followed. She had a sense that they were. She was beginning to feel very uneasy.

After more walking, Lucy suddenly began sniffing the air.

'What is it Lucy?' asked Gabriella.

'Smoke, I can smell smoke.'

They all sniffed and there was now a much stronger smell of smoke. Gabriella flew on ahead to investigate. Within minutes she was back.

'There's a cottage and it's in a clearing not far from here. Whoever lives there has a fire going and there is a light in the window.'

'I hope they're friendly,' said Ellie. 'It's almost too dark to see. If it wasn't for your fairy glow Gabriella we couldn't have got this far.'

'I hope they've got some food and will share it with us,' said Lucy, holding her tummy.

The three friends trekked through the wood and out into the clearing. The moon was hidden behind thick clouds. The cottage was very small and more like a shed than a house. There was one window but they couldn't see inside because curtains were drawn over it.

'Well, here goes,' said Ellie and she knocked on the door.

The door was opened by a beautiful young woman in a long green and brown gown. She had long golden hair and looked far too elegant to be living in such a place.

'Hello,' she said, smiling at them. 'Are you lost? Come in.'

'Thank you,' said Lucy, as they entered the cottage. When they looked around, the place seemed much bigger on the inside than it could possibly be from the outside. It was very cosy too. The woman laughed gently at their amazement.

'Fairy magic,' she said. 'Do sit down.'

They sat around the lovely warm fire on chairs made of wood and soft green moss, draped with silken material.

'Are you a fairy then?' asked Ellie noticing that she didn't have any visible wings.

'No, not really. I'm a dryad. I live in the woods most of the time, but sometimes I come here for a little extra warmth and comfort. I see one of you is a fairy. What are you two, if you don't mind me asking?'

'We're humans,' said Ellie. 'We've come here to…'

'To visit Fairyland with our friend,' Lucy interrupted. She didn't think it wise to give anything away just yet.

'Are you hungry?' the dryad asked, looking at Lucy.

Lucy nodded. 'We're starving. Well, I am anyway.'

'Well then, we woodland folk are renowned for our hospitality. Let me go and prepare something for you.' The dryad went into the kitchen.

'Wow, this place is amazing. I thought we'd all be squashed round a little fire, with no room to spare,' said Ellie.

'She is beautiful isn't she?' said Lucy.

'Yes,' said Gabriella. 'Dryads are very rare creatures. Not usually hospitable to strangers actually, they prefer to keep to their own kind.'

'Oh that is true,' said the dryad returning from the kitchen. 'But we are not unkind either. I couldn't leave you out there all night, could I?' she said, giving Gabriella a not very smiley smile. 'Now, come, eat and drink. Then you need sleep I would think. You've come a long way.'

The three friends looked at each other, then hunger took over and they tucked in. 'This is lovely, thank you,' said Gabriella, rather embarrassed that her comments had been overheard.

'You are all most welcome,' said the dryad.

When they had eaten food that tasted like a banquet they did feel very sleepy, sitting by the warm fire.

'Come, I will find you beds to sleep in and then in the morning we can get to know each other.'

The dryad led them to another room with three beds beautifully made up for them. They thanked her and fell exhausted into the beds.

'Sleep well friends,' said the dryad closing the door.

The next morning, when they awoke there was a lovely smell of cooking drifting through the cottage. 'Good morning,' said the dryad as they emerged from the bedroom. I'm sure you slept well. Come and eat.'

There was freshly made bread, cinnamon toast and eggs, washed down with a warm sweet drink that tasted like honey and milk.

'So how may I help you?' asked the dryad, even though no one had asked for her help.

Lucy spoke. 'We are trying to find out what has been happening in Fairyland recently. Our fairy friend has been staying with us for a while and things seem a little odd since we have returned.'

The dryad looked at Gabriella. 'And what is your name, dear fairy friend?'

'Erm... well ...' she looked at Ellie, 'It's Gabriella.'

For a brief moment a look of shock passed across the dryad's face. Then she regained her smile.

'And your friends?'

'Ellie and Lucy,' Gabriella said. 'Do you know anything about what has been happening?'

'I can tell you that you are not in Elysia.'

'Elysia?' said Ellie.

'Yes, Gabriella's kingdom, I mean, where she comes from. Hasn't she told you about it? We are in the Borderlands between Elysia and Morteribus.'

Everyone turned to Gabriella. She had her eyes closed.

'What is wrong with your friend?' whispered the dryad.

'She is missing her home,' Lucy said quickly. 'She is probably imagining it right now.'

'What's your name?' asked Ellie.

'My name is Silveria. I am a silver birch dryad.'

'Nice to meet you. You've been really kind to us,' said Ellie. 'We could do with some help to find our way back to Elysia, if you wouldn't mind.'

'I'd be happy to escort you,' smiled Silveria.

Gabriella opened her eyes.

'Silveria is going to help us find our way to Elysia,' Ellie said.

'Oh thank you.' Gabriella's eyes sparkled. 'Elysia is such a beautiful place.'

'Yes,' said Silveria with a strange smile. 'Shall we go?'

Chapter Seven

The River

The dryad led the way through the clearing and back into the woods. This time it was light and she knew her way skilfully through the trees. But the forest still seemed as if it was watching them. There was an eerie feeling about it. After about an hour of walking they came to a river. There was no bridge in sight but a boat was tied to a jetty.

'You must cross the river to get into Elysia. The boatman will take you,' said Silveria.

They had not seen a boatman but when they looked down into the boat again there he was. A small creature in a hooded cloak. No one could see his face. Silveria stepped back from the shore.

'Aren't you coming with us?' asked Gabriella.

'No, I cannot. You must go alone now. Goodbye.'

The dryad turned and walked back towards the wood. As she did so, the boatman beckoned them with a long bony finger. As the three stepped into the boat, the boatman threw off his hood. Gabriella screamed and tried to fly up from the boat, but she couldn't. There seemed to be something holding her down. At once, magic ropes began to slither around the three friends. They were held fast in the boat. Ellie and Lucy struggled, but it was useless.

'Help!' Help! Silveria, help us!' Ellie shouted. But Sliveria had vanished into the trees.

'She led us into a trap,' Lucy said.

The Goblin chuckled. 'She had no choice.'

'It's you!' gasped Gabriella. 'You're the one who tried to … kill me.'

'That is true,' he replied, as he began to row the boat out into the river. 'But you didn't die. I presume these humans rescued you. Well, they're going to be sorry they did.'

Lucy held on tightly to Ellie. Ellie held on tightly to Lucy.

'We'll never be sorry we rescued her,' said Ellie, trying not to let her voice quiver. 'What has she done to you anyway?'

'Nothing to me, personally,' he replied, 'but my master does not want the princess trying to claim her throne when he has turned her parents into hobgoblin slaves.'

'Princess?' Gabriella gasped.

'Don't pretend you're not the princess. I know you. I kidnapped you from the palace. Now you will join your parents in my master's dungeon. You and your human friends will be turned into hobgoblin slaves. My master is going to be ruler of Elysia soon.'

Lucy began to cry quietly and Ellie shivered. She would have to think of a way to escape. She held Lucy's hand tightly. 'Don't worry,' Ellie whispered, 'We'll think of something.'

Lucy nodded and tried to smile.

'I'm sorry I brought you to this,' said Gabriella.

'I'm not,' said Ellie. 'We're not going to let them take your kingdom.'

The Goblin laughed. 'You're too late for that, little human. Our goblins are already swarming into Elysia. The fairies have been put under a powerful spell by my master and none of them is powerful enough to break it.' He glanced worriedly at Gabriella. Then he snorted. 'You are useless in this world, human. Now, be quiet – all of you.'

The boat ploughed on through the water. It was very quiet apart from the splash of the oars and the goblin muttering strange words to himself and chuckling now and then. A mist was descending over the river and the birds were no longer singing. It began to get cold. The three friends sat in silence for some time: all of them trying to think of a way to escape. Gabriella could not get her arms free in order to do any fairy magic. Then Ellie remembered that in her pocket she had her dad's penknife. If she could get to it she could cut the ropes. She squirmed and twisted when the goblin wasn't looking. Lucy and Gabriella gave her a *what-are-you-doing?* look. She got her hands to her pocket and felt the knife. Opening it out was tricky but she managed it. Then she twisted her wrist into a position that was quite painful and started to hack at the rope. Whenever the goblin looked her way she sat perfectly still and pretended to be staring out at the river. At last Ellie felt her rope come lose. She pushed the knife into Gabriella's hands. Gabriella cut steadily through her rope, then it was Lucy's turn. Using only their eyes and small head gestures, the three friends communicated their plan to each other.

Suddenly Ellie shouted, 'Now!'

The three of them grabbed at the goblin and heaved him out of the boat. It all happened so fast that he didn't have time to do any magic. Once he had plopped into the water Gabriella flung fairy dust at him, putting a spell on him to keep him from getting out of the water. Then she sank back into the boat from the effort. Ellie and Lucy grabbed the oars and heaved with all their might.

'You won't get away,' he screeched. 'My master will find you.'

'Shall I try some magic to make the boat row itself?' asked Gabriella.

'Don't be silly,' said Ellie. 'You've got no strength left. We can do it, can't we Lucy?'

'Yes,' gasped Lucy, heaving on the oars with all her might.

'My spell on the goblin might wear off quickly. I don't think it was very powerful,' said Gabriella.

'Don't worry,' Lucy said, 'We'll get away. Ellie and I are a good team.' She smiled at Ellie. Then turning again to Gabriella, she said, 'You need to rest.' But Gabriella's eyes were already closed.

The girls rowed until their whole bodies ached. They felt very cold too. They didn't know where they were rowing to and the mist made it difficult to see.

'They'll be worried about us at home,' said Ellie.

'Maybe they won't have missed us,' said Lucy. 'It could be like in some stories where the people go into another world but don't use up any time in their own.'

'It's weird to think I didn't believe in any of this 'til I met Gabriella,' said Ellie. 'No one back home would believe us.'

'I hope we get back home,' said Lucy in a small voice.

'We will,' Ellie reassured her, hoping that she was right. 'Together, whatever, remember.'

'Together, whatever,' Lucy said, managing a faint smile.

A huge black shadow loomed out of the mist over the river. It was a bridge. As the boat passed under it a voice said, 'You're heading the wrong way.' It was an old man's voice.

Lucy shouted up. 'Who's there? And how do you know that?'

The old man said,' Row your boat to the shore. There's a jetty up ahead. That fairy needs help.'

Gabriella was still asleep. The girls wondered how the old man could see her in the mist.

'What shall we do?' Ellie whispered. 'We've only met bad people so far.'

'I know you don't trust me yet but you will. You'll never help the King and Queen if you don't,' the voice said.

'I think we should do it,' said Lucy. 'He seems to know more about what we're doing and where we're going than we do.'

'Ok, but let's be careful.'

Chapter Eight

Perizam

They landed the boat by the jetty and woke Gabriella. 'Come on Gabriella. Can you stand?'

Shakily, she got to her feet and out of the boat with Lucy and Ellie's help. 'Where are we?'

'You are in the Borderlands close to the edge of Morteribus,' came the voice. A small, round man emerged from the mist. His face was wizened and his arms and legs were short. He wore a woollen bobble hat. Ellie thought he looked like a walking pumpkin. He carried a fishing line and two silver fish that were nearly as long as himself. 'Follow me,' he said, turning to waddle across the field.

The three friends looked at each other and followed at a distance.

'Who is he?' asked Gabriella.

'We don't know, but he seems to know something about us,' whispered Lucy.

They came to a small wooden building, not unlike Sliveria's cottage on the outside. The friends hesitated. The man opened the door and went inside. When they didn't follow he peered back around the door.

'Come in before you freeze.'

Inside, it was not like Silveria's magical cottage. It was really small and it was a squash to fit them all in. There was only one room with a kitchen area at one end and in the middle a sofa by the fire. A bed was at the other end of the room. The man lit the fire and made them all a warm drink, which tasted woody but sweet. No one spoke for some time. The girls warmed themselves and the man busied himself preparing the fish he had caught. Soon they were all tucking into the most delicious meal.

As they ate they glanced shyly at the creature. He never once looked up from his fish. Gabriella had a strange look on her face as if she was remembering something.

'Should I know you?' she asked at last. ' I feel like I do, but I've lost my memory.'

For the first time the little man smiled. His whole face lit up and at once the girls felt at ease.

'Princess Gabriella,' he said, 'I feared you were lost forever.'

'But, my name's not really Gabriella,' she said. 'Ellie just picked the name for me because I couldn't remember mine.'

He smiled at Ellie this time. 'You, young human, chose her own name because, although she didn't know it, it was written in her eyes all the time.'

Ellie raised her eyebrows and shrugged. She was sure she had just picked the name of a pop star from a poster.

'These are my friends Ellie and Lucy. Without them I would not have got back to Fairyland.'

'We owe you much,' said the man, nodding at Lucy and Ellie.

'What is your name?' asked Gabriella.

'I am Perizam. I have known you since you were born, Princess. Your father and I knew each other from childhood. We were the oddest friends you've ever seen.' He chuckled. 'And then your mother chose him to be her prince and I got to know her too. What a beautiful fairy she is.' He sighed. 'You look so like her my dear.'

'Where are they? What has happened?'

'More holmi?' asked Perizam, holding up the teapot.

They all had more to drink and Perizam began to tell them what had happened.

'Your parents are Queen Hermia and Prince Lysander of Elysia. You are an only child. Elysia was a beautiful kingdom: a place of crystal streams, majestic waterfalls and beautiful flowers. The rain was refreshing; the sun was warm and pleasant. However, the ruler of Morteribus, the neighbouring kingdom, is evil. His name is Maleaver. He has always wanted to rule Elysia. So he kidnapped you and your parents and spread a powerful magic over the fairies in Elysia. Now Elysia has lost its sparkle. The fairies don't fly anymore or create colourful magic. Not because they can't, but because the spell on them means they don't want to, they can't be bothered. Other creatures have also been affected by it.'

'Like Silveria, the dryad?' asked Ellie.

'Yes. She was a beautiful dryad leader but Maleaver wanted her to be his queen. So he put her under a spell and now she does his bidding. Maleaver was going to turn you and your parents into hobgoblin slaves, as part of a big ceremony to crown him Ruler of Elysia. However, you, my dear, escaped.'

'And I came here for help,' said Gabriella.

'You did.' Perizam smiled as he looked into Gabriella's eyes and saw her memory seeping back.

'But the night after you arrived the goblins came. They overpowered us both and ran off with you. That goblin in the boat is called Grizzle. He is Maleaver's henchman.'

'What's a henchman?' asked Lucy.

'Someone sent to get rid of people, to kill them usually. You did very well to surprise him in the boat like that.'

Lucy shivered.

'Have you been following us?' asked Ellie.

'In a way, yes. I felt your arrival in the woods. I was surprised and relieved that the princess was still alive.'

'Felt it?' said Ellie.

'Perizam has a gift of knowledge. He sometimes knows what is happening without being able to see it,' said Gabriella, her face lighting up as she was able to remember things.

'In my mind I have followed you. I knew we would meet here but I thought I'd have to help you tackle Grizzle. You surprised me there.'

'So, where are my parents?'

'Maleaver has them locked up in the dungeon of his castle. In two days time he plans to set off for Elysia to claim his crown and turn them into his slaves.'

'We must stop him,' said Ellie immediately. 'He can't get away with that.'

'You are a brave one, my dear,' said Perizam. 'I know you were brought here to protect the princess.'

'We need a plan,' Lucy put in.

'And you, little one, you are the thinker eh?' He chuckled. 'You are a good team.'

'My magic is not working very well,' said Gabriella. 'Each time I do some magic, I feel exhausted.'

'I know Princess. Grizzle did a terrible thing to you. However, it will return, given time, just like your memory is beginning to. When we finally see some moonlight, it will help. I think it's part of the bad magic that has settled over the land.'

Everyone was silent for a time. Then Perizam said, 'We all need some sleep. In the morning we can decide what to do. For now, you are safe from harm.'

Somehow they all managed to find a place in which to sleep. Perizam gave up his bed for Princess Gabriella even though she protested. He insisted. It was quite small but Gabriella curled up on her side and was asleep in no time. Ellie and Lucy were given blankets and cushions. They were so exhausted that they could have slept on a park bench. Perizam pulled his coat over himself and slept in his armchair next to the dying fire.

Chapter Nine

Setting Out

The next morning was as grey as the last, though not quite as misty. Ellie woke with a churning feeling in her stomach. It was like the feeling you get when you've got a hard spelling test at school and you know you haven't been learning the words. Lucy and Gabriella were still asleep, but Perizam was nowhere to be seen. Ellie decided to get some fresh air. As she stepped outside, Perizam was coming towards her with four more fish in his hands.

'Breakfast,' he said. 'Are you rested?'

'Yes thank you. We were very tired with all that rowing yesterday.'

Perizam regarded her with a worried look. Then he smiled. 'We should wake the others and decide what we are going to do.'

Gabriella was already awake but Lucy was still fast asleep and very difficult to wake.

'This little one is worn out,' said Perizam, looking worried again.

Eventually they woke Lucy, who seemed remarkably cheerful. Over breakfast they discussed their plans.

'I can take you to Maleaver's castle, but I'm not sure how we will get in,' said Perizam. 'I know it is heavily guarded. Grizzle is on his way back there now with news of your escape. They will be watching for you and may even send out a band of goblins to look for you.'

'Can they do magic like fairies?' asked Lucy.

'They have limited magic,' said Gabriella. 'Like the ropes in Grizzle's boat.'

'Sometimes they can be granted extra powers for certain tasks,' Perizam added. 'Like when Grizzle tried to kill the princess. Fortunately his magic didn't succeed.'

'Is your magic more powerful?' Ellie asked Gabriella.

'Yes, when it is restored.'

'She is a fairy princess. She should have very powerful magic. Maleaver of course also possesses very powerful magic. He somehow managed to overpower the Queen and Prince Lysander. They are imprisoned in a dungeon, which prevents any magic from being used.'

'Well, we will fight the goblins if we have to,' said Ellie.

Perizam looked doubtful. 'I know you were sent to protect Princess Gabriella, but you are human and possess no magic.'

'Yes, but she is great at standing up to bullies,' said Lucy, grinning at Ellie. 'And we will help her …somehow.'

Ellie smiled back at Lucy. She didn't feel confident at all of being able to overpower the goblins.

'We need a way past the guards,' said Lucy. They all sat deep in thought for some time.

'We should just go,' said Gabriella. 'We can think on the way.'

They packed a few things that might be of use and a little food. There was not much talking as they all thought about what lay ahead. It was hard going, through wet fields and dark woods. Everything was cloaked in an eerie mist, which made them feel damp, cold and wary. Perizam was a good guide. He seemed to know the way and never hesitated in choosing which direction to take.

'Can we rest for a while?' asked Lucy.

'Of course child,' said Perizam. The others were glad of the rest too, although Perizam, despite his small legs, never seemed to grow weary. Gabriella had been walking with the others, saving her energy in case she might need it later.

As they sat together Perizam said quietly, 'We are being followed. They are not far behind us. We can't stay here long. We must cross the river up ahead and there is no bridge. There maybe be a boat left by one of the woodland folk, otherwise we will have to swim. Are you ready?'

They nodded. Ellie wondered how on earth someone of Perizam's shape would be able to swim. She hoped there was a boat. They tried to walk faster but it was difficult with Perizam leading them. His legs were not made for striding. Lucy and Ellie kept looking behind them. At the moment, they could neither see nor hear anyone. Gabriella was trying to quicken the pace. She kept fluttering up into the air.

'I can see the river ahead,' she said, coming down. It's just over the next rise.

Suddenly Lucy cried,' Look! Goblins! Coming out of the woods!' A group of about six or seven had begun to run towards them.

'Run!' yelled Ellie.

Even Perizam began to run. The girls and the fairy tried to pull him along. Gabriella was flying above. She lifted him by the coat and the girls grabbed his arms. Between them they lifted him off the ground and carried him like a big beach ball with little legs dangling below. If they hadn't been so frightened, Ellie thought they would have been in fits of giggles now, at how ridiculous they must look.

The goblins were gaining on them as they reached the river. They stopped, puffing and panting, their eyes searching for a boat.

'We're out of luck,' Gabriella panted. 'Looks like you're swimming. I will have to fly because I can't swim. I would carry you in turn but...'

'We haven't got time,' said Ellie, let's go!' She plunged into the river. It was freezing, but she stopped herself from shrieking. Perizam plunged in after her. Amazingly he powered along on top of the water, his legs acting as propellers. Lucy looked doubtfully at the river. Then she glanced even more doubtfully at the goblins getting closer and threw herself into the water. The river was flowing the way they were heading but they had to battle to cross it. Gabriella had reached the other shore and was shouting encouragements at them.

The goblins reached the shore. Ellie saw that Grizzle was their leader. There was a carriage behind them, being pulled by two captured unicorns. Someone stepped out of the carriage. Gabriella could see it was not a goblin at all. It was a tall, beautiful woman. Silveria!

'Come on!' Gabriella cried to her friends who were battling against the current. Ellie was nearly there and Perizam was not far behind. As Ellie climbed out on the other shore she looked back and saw Lucy in some difficulty.

'I'm going back for her,' she told Gabriella.

Lucy was being swept away with the tide. She kept going under. Ellie had just got her 400 metres badge in swimming last week. This was very different to a swimming pool though.

'Lucy!' she shouted. 'I'm coming, try to tread water.'

To Gabriella's horror she saw the goblins drawing out bows and arrows. 'Fire!' commanded Sliveria. Arrows zipped through the air.

'Take cover Princess,' shouted Perizam, who had just climbed out of the river. He tried to shield her with his little round body. 'Run to those trees over there.'

'No,' Gabriella cried,' I have to help Ellie and Lucy.'

The arrows came fast and furious. Some dropped into the water near Ellie and Lucy. They fizzled and sank. However, it was clear that Gabriella was the target.

'Buffoons!' cried Sliveria. 'Who taught you to shoot? Give that to me.'

She pushed Grizzle to the floor and snatched his bow. Carefully, she took aim. Her arrow sped like a magnet to metal. It was not like a normal arrow. It was magic because, as it made contact with Gabriella, it put out claws and grabbed her. Then a silver rope appeared, attached to it, and drew Gabriella through the air towards Silveria. Gabriella screamed and twisted trying to break free, but her arms were firmly grasped so she could not do any magic.

'No!' cried Perizam.

'We have her!' shouted Grizzle.

Ellie had just got to Lucy. 'I've got you Lucy. Kick your legs as hard as you can.' She pulled at the frightened Lucy's arm. She could see what had happened to Gabriella. Ellie heaved Lucy onto the shore. 'I'm going back,' she said.

Perizam put his hand on her arm. 'No child, it is not your time yet.' Ellie didn't understand what that meant, but as she turned, she saw the carriage speeding away with the goblins running alongside and behind it. They were laughing and whooping. They had their prize.

'We have to do something,' Ellie protested.

'We will,' said Perizam. 'But first we must sort ourselves out. Silveria and the goblins will have to cross the river up ahead. When they do we will catch up with them.'

'How will they cross the river?' asked Lucy, who was shivering on the shore.

'The unicorns will easily pull the carriage through the river. The goblins will have to swim.'

'How will we catch them? They have unicorns and a carriage. We are on foot and we're slow,' said Ellie.

'I have some money. Maybe someone will sell us a horse. Come we must go on. Let's try and find shelter for the night and get you dried.'

Lucy smiled bravely at Perizam. They set off to walk some more.

Chapter Ten

Chasing Goblins

It was very late when they came across a small settlement of woodland folk. Perizam knocked at a door. A thin old woman came to the door. She was bent over and had to turn her face up to look at the girls.

'Who are you? What do you want?'

Perizam spoke. 'Good lady, we are travellers, seeking warmth and a bed for the night. We can pay.'

She eyed them suspiciously. 'No one up to any good travels these days. Too dangerous.'

'I assure you we mean you no harm. Would this help?' Perizam drew out of his drawstring purse some small silver coins.

The woman reached out to touch them. She hesitated. 'Come in then, quickly.' She looked up and down the street, then shut the door. 'There's bad creatures in the Borderlands lately,' she said. 'Sit down. You can have some soup.'

'Thank you,' said Perizam. 'My friends here are wet and cold. Is there a place they could dry their clothes?'

She looked at the shivering girls as if she had not really noticed them before. They tried to smile at her. The woman's voice was sharp and suspicious. 'What creatures are you? You don't look like woodland children.'

'We're hu…'

Lucy interrupted. 'We're just friends of Perizam: From a different part of Fairyland.'

'Well come with me and put your clothes to dry. I have blankets you can put round yourselves.'

Soon the girls sat in warm blankets by the fire with Perizam. The woman busied herself with soup. 'Can I help?' asked Lucy. 'I'd like to. You've been very kind to us.'

A tiny smile appeared like another crack in the old woman's worn face. 'You are a thoughtful one.' Lucy laid the small table with bread and berries, spoons and cups. The woman brought bowls of steaming soup to the table.

'This is lovely,' said Ellie, with a mouthful of bread. They were all very hungry.

'You make delicious soup,' added Perizam, smiling at the woman. She smiled back, beginning to warm to her guests.

'Do you know anyone who might sell us a horse?' asked Perizam.

'Are you going far then?' she asked.

'Yes. A horse would be a very welcome addition to our party.'

'My neighbour keeps horses. I'll ask him in the morning. Now these children look exhausted. Let's find you all a place to sleep.'

The house was small but the woman did have a spare room. There was no bed in there so Lucy and Ellie curled up together on a rug to keep warm. They were getting used to sleeping on the ground. Perizam slept in the living room.

'Ellie,' said Lucy. 'Do you think we can really save Gabriella? It seems impossible. I really want to go home now.'

Ellie hugged her. 'I think we can help her, Lucy. Then we'll go home. I promise. Trust me, I won't let anything bad happen to you.'

Lucy cuddled in to her friend and they soon fell asleep.

The next morning, the girls were woken by Perizam gently shaking them. 'I have a horse. We need to go.'

The girls got up and dressed. Their clothes were now dry.

They thanked the woman and Lucy even gave her a kiss on the cheek. The woman seemed very pleased about that. 'Now you go carefully, do you hear?'

'We will,' said Lucy. The woman waved as they headed up the street to collect their new horse. 'I can ride,' said Lucy. 'I go for lessons back home.' She tried not to let her eyes fill up at the thought of home, swiping angrily at them.

'That will be useful then,' said Perizam. 'What about you child?' he said to Ellie.

'I've never ridden anything except donkeys at the seaside.'

'You'll be ok. I'll show you the basics,' said Lucy with some pride in her voice.

'What about you Perizam?' said Ellie, looking at his shape and wondering how on earth he would get his little legs over a horse.

'I have bought us a little cart, which the horse will pull easily. I shall ride in that.'

The horse was a lovely chestnut brown. He was quite big and Ellie looked worried. They had to ride him bareback but Lucy gave Ellie some tips. Ellie climbed awkwardly onto the horse's back and Lucy climbed up behind her. The cart was attached and they set off. They were all grateful not to have to walk.

'They are not too far ahead of us,' said Perizam. 'If we don't rest for long we will catch them. They will make camp for the night when they cross into Morteribus. Then it is only another day's journey to Maleaver's castle.'

'I have an idea,' said Lucy, when they had stopped for a short rest and to let the horse drink. 'If we can free Gabriella when the goblins are sleeping, she could use her magic to release Silveria from the enchantment she is under. But Silveria could pretend that she was still under the spell. She could make the goblins believe

they had captured us, so we could get into the castle. She could help us find the Queen and Prince.'

'But even if she is released from the enchantment, she may not want to help us. She may just want to escape,' said Ellie.

'Silveria is a dryad. Dryads are loyal to Queen Hermia. She will help us,' said Perizam. Then he added, 'It will use a lot of Princess Gabriella's energy to break the enchantment.'

'It's worth a try, isn't it?' said Lucy.

They agreed it was.

Through the afternoon they made good progress. Lucy had always imagined Fairyland to be a colourful, sunny place, with pretty fairies flitting around and beautiful things to look at. This place was not at all like the picture she had painted in her mind. Ellie had never imagined Fairyland, not having believed in fairies until now. The dark emptiness of this place made her feel trapped. She too thought of home and wondered if they would ever return. She, like Lucy, was afraid, but one thing was certain in their minds: they would not abandon Gabriella.

As the daylight faded it became much colder. The old woman had given them blankets for their journey, which they wrapped round themselves.

'We have crossed into Morteribus,' said Perizam. 'We must be more careful who sees us. It is not far now. They have set up camp just beyond that hill, in the hollow. We must wait until those foolish goblins sleep and hope that Silveria sleeps too.'

'Won't they set a guard on Gabriella?' asked Ellie.

'Yes, but goblins are not very reliable.'

The three travellers stopped just beneath the brow of the hill. They crept on their stomachs to look down into the camp. Ellie almost giggled as she remembered playing commandos with Calllum. Then the reality of where she was took away any feelings of merriment. It was very late but they could hear voices and laughing. The hollow was dotted with trees, which would be good for hiding behind. There was a campfire and Ellie thought she could see Gabriella tied to a tree a little way off from the others. There was a guard sitting not very far away from her. No one could see Silveria though.

'Is Silveria there, Perizam?'

'I feel her presence but I can't see her.'

There was no sign of the goblins going to sleep. They were getting noisier, until the door of the carriage opened and Silveria appeared.

'Be quiet you fools!' she shouted. 'Are you trying to attract attention to us?'

The goblins quietened to a murmur and Silveria went back inside the carriage. Ellie and Lucy were finding it hard to keep their eyes open despite being afraid of what they were about to do. The next thing they knew was Perizam gently shaking them awake.

'It is quiet down there now. They are drunk on goblin grog. This is our chance.'

Ellie and Lucy looked fearfully at each other. Then Ellie put her hand out, palm down. Lucy understood and put hers on top. Perizam was not quite sure what was going on but he followed the pattern. Then they repeated it, one hand on top of the other.

Together, whatever!' Ellie whispered.

'Together whatever!' the others repeated.

Chapter Eleven

The Rescue

They crept down the slope on their hands and knees, trying to keep in the shadows. There was still no moon, but the stars gave some light. As they reached the edge of the camp they could see and hear shapes snoring on the ground. Lucy glanced at the carriage, hoping that Silveria was also asleep. Ellie looked around for Gabriella. She could see her, still asleep against the tree, perilously close to Silveria's carriage. There was a goblin near her. It was Grizzle, but he was slumped over a tree stump, which hopefully meant he was asleep too.

'We have to try not to startle her, or she might scream,' Lucy whispered.

They stood up and walked as softly as they could through the camp, trying not to cause any noise. They crept round the sleeping goblins but Ellie stumbled into one. She froze.

'Wazzabizzazaza...' he mumbled, then he was snoring again.

Ellie heaved a sigh of relief and tried to be more careful. Even in the cold night air she could feel sweat trickling down her back. As they approached Gabriella, Perizam could see that she was asleep. He walked in front of her and gently put his hand over her mouth. Her eyes opened wide and as soon as he was sure she knew it was him, he took his hand away.

'I knew you'd come,' she whispered.

'Quick, let's untie you,' said Ellie.

'Are you all right?' asked Lucy.

'Just shaken and cold,' said Gabriella.

Ellie fiddled with the rope but it wouldn't come undone. Lucy tried, but every time she thought she was releasing the knot, it seemed to tie itself even tighter.

'Its magic rope,' said Gabriella. 'You probably can't untie it.'

'My dad's knife,' said Ellie. She still had it in her pocket. She sawed at the rope but this time, it would not cut.

'What are we going to do?' asked Lucy.

'Put your knife by one of my hands, Ellie,' said Gabriella.

Gabriella's arms were tied round the tree. She could hardly move her hands. She wiggled her fingers over the knife.

'It just might work,' she said.

A tiny amount of fairy dust glowed in the dark and sprinkled over the knife. 'Now try it.'

Ellie sliced through the rope as easily as if it had been a piece of string.

At that moment there was a noise from the carriage. The door began to open. The three rescuers darted round the back. Gabriella closed her eyes again and hoped the rope still looked secure. Silveria stepped out and looked around. She glanced at Gabriella then marched over to Grizzle, who was snoring, and pushed him off the stump.

'Wake up, buffoon! If we don't get her to Maleaver both our heads will be removed from our bodies. Now guard her. If you sleep again I will tie you up and leave you here to be eaten by wolves when we leave.'

The goblin pulled himself to attention as best he could and stumbled closer to Gabriella. Silveria retreated to her carriage. Ellie, Lucy and Perizam held their breath. Grizzle was approaching Gabriella. Surely he would see that the rope was hanging loose around the tree. Ellie got ready to pounce. Grizzle bent down to check on Gabriella. Just at that moment she flung her arms towards him and showered him with fairy dust. All he could do was cough and in an instant he was tied to the tree and unable to speak. His mouth kept opening and closing but no sound came out. The others crept out from behind the carriage.

'Phew, that was close!' said Lucy, still careful to keep her voice down.

'Are you all right, Princess?' asked Perizam

'I am now,' said Gabriella, but she staggered and Ellie caught her before she fell.

'That magic has taken all your energy again,' said Ellie.

'And I don't know how long it will last,' said Gabriella.

They looked at Grizzle who was struggling and silently shouting for help.

'We'll have to change our plan,' said Lucy, moving them all away from Grizzle, whose ears were still working. 'Gabriella won't have enough magic now to break Silveria's enchantment. She needs to rest first.'

'I think a kidnap is in order,' said Perizam. 'If we can get the unicorns to help us by pulling the carriage again, we could get away with Silveria. The goblins would pursue us but it would give Gabriella time to recover and try to break the enchantment.'

'Then we could let them think they've caught us and the plan would kick in again,' said Lucy.

'You have it child,' said Perizam.

'We'll have to hurry and hitch up the unicorns ever so quietly,' said Ellie.

'Let's try it. Perizam and I will talk to the unicorns and get them hitched up. You two guard the carriage door. If she comes out, pounce on her. Don't let her raise her hands to do any magic.'

The unicorns were very willing to help a fairy princess and quietly they backed towards the carriage. As they were hitched up, the carriage moved slightly and there was some noise. Just as they were ready to move, Silveria stirred. The door of the carriage began to open.

'Quick,' said Ellie. She jumped at Silveria and knocked her back inside the carriage. 'Get in!' she yelled. Lucy, Gabriella and Perizam hurled themselves into the carriage.

'Go my friends, go!' Perizam shouted to the unicorns. 'As fast as you can.'

By this time the drunken goblins around the fire were moving. They rubbed their eyes sleepily and several of them grumbled about being woken up. Suddenly, one of them realised that the carriage was speeding away. At the same moment another saw that Gabriella was gone.

'Quick, after it!' shouted a goblin.

'They began running after the carriage. But it was still dark and they tripped and stumbled. One fell over Grizzle, who was tied to the tree. He tried to release him but couldn't undo the magic rope. Eventually he realised why. He found a magic wand and released Grizzle.

'We've got to catch them,' said Grizzle, the silent magic having worn off. 'I can't let them escape again. And they have Silveria.' The goblin pack ran clumsily through the dark after the carriage.

Inside the carriage everyone was being thrown around as the unicorns ran with great speed. All of them, except Gabriella, were piled on top of Silveria in a big heap, desperate to stop her doing any magic. Silveria was struggling hard to get free and shouting at them.

'You'll never get away with this. Don't you know Maleaver will find you? I am to be his queen, and you will be his slaves.'

'Be quiet, Silveria,' Gabriella said. She was slumped on the seat trying to get some energy back to break the enchantment. She knew it would take some doing. 'Don't you care that you are harming fairies and all that is good in this land?'

'Why should I care? I am going to be very powerful with Maleaver's help.'

'But you are a dryad. Dryads and fairies have been friends forever.'

'Get these fools off me!' Silveria yelled.

'You are under a bad enchantment Silveria. We are going to help you,' said Gabriella.

'Nonsense. I am doing this because I want to be second in command of the whole of Fairyland. And with Maleaver's help I will be.'

'Don't let her go,' said Gabriella. 'I should be able to try soon.'

'Try what?' said Silveria.

'To help you,' replied Gabriella.

Chapter Twelve

Breaking the Enchantment

The unicorns slowed to a trot once they knew that the goblins were not about to catch them. It was a very difficult task keeping Silveria down. Finally, she gave up struggling and lay still, but the others did not get off her. She grumbled and tried to lash out now and again, but they were determined to hold her. It felt to Ellie like being in a wrestling match. Karate was far easier than this.

After a while, the unicorns stopped to drink. They were well into Morteribus now and it was morning; although the light was very pale and watery. There was no visible sun and the mist that had been following them was even thicker. Each person in turn went outside to drink from the spring, with the unicorns, while the others held Silveria down. When Gabriella returned to the carriage she felt ready to try and break the enchantment. However, she could not do it with the others piled on top of Silveria. She needed all of her fairy dust to land on Silveria. She would have to take a chance.

'Silveria,' she said, feeling much more in charge of the situation than she had ever done before, 'We are going to release you on one condition. You let me try to break the enchantment that is on you. If, as you say, there is no such enchantment, then nothing will change in you and we will be your prisoners. But if I am right, then you will thank me for saving you from Maleaver's evil scheme.'

Silveria grumbled, but she wanted to be free from the heavy bodies pinning her down, so she agreed. Ellie didn't trust her one little bit and got ready to pounce on her at the slightest movement. But they released her and she sat up in the seat opposite Gabriella. The fairy gathered all her strength and said some strange fairy words. She pointed her fingers at Silveria and released a storm cloud of fairy dust towards her. Silveria closed her eyes and gasped. Then she slumped forward into a deep sleep. Ellie and Perizam just caught her before she fell off the seat.

'Lay her down,' said Gabriella, 'she will need to rest. When she comes round she should be restored.' At this, Gabriella closed her eyes and fell back in a faint.

'You must rest too, Princess,' said Perizam, touching her head. Ellie and Lucy lifted her feet up onto the seat. Then the three friends stepped out of the carriage.

'We should wait a while,' Perizam said. 'The goblins need time to catch us up.'

'I hope Silveria will wake up before they get here,' said Lucy.

'And I hope she is free from the enchantment,' said Ellie.

Perizam suggested they make a fire while they wait. So they collected firewood and soon there was a warm blaze to keep out the chill of this awful place. The girls told Perizam about life in their world. They talked about school and their families and hobbies. Eventually, they all lapsed into silence, as they longed for happier times.

It wasn't long before the door of the carriage opened and Silveria stepped out. She looked exactly the same. They held their breath for fear that she might not have changed. She came over to the fire, her tall figure towering above them. Then, to their surprise, she knelt in front of Perizam.

'Dear Perizam, thank you.' She took his small, nobbly fingers in her long slim hand and kissed them. He blushed so much that he looked like a rosy red apple. Ellie and Lucy began to giggle.

'And you, Ellie and Lucy, I thank you. You have helped the princess so much and saved me from a terrible fate.'

She stood up and bent to kiss them on the foreheads. They knew that she was free from the enchantment and began to tell her of their plan.

'The goblins will be here very soon,' warned Perizam. 'Silveria, you need to pretend we are your prisoners.'

'What about the princess?' she asked. 'She still lies in an exhausted sleep.'

'You must tie us all up. She will understand when she comes round,' said Perizam.

Silveria tied them up, with magic rope, in the carriage, then she sat outside near the dying fire, to await the arrival of the goblins.

It wasn't long before the goblins appeared. They were making such a noise, grumbling and squabbling, that they could be heard before they could be seen. Silveria took a deep breath and stood up.

'You fools!' she bellowed. 'How did you let them kidnap me? And how has it taken so long to find us? You are lucky that I am strong and was easily able to overpower the weak little creatures. More than can be said for you!'

'They tricked us Silveria. We couldn't help it,' whined one of the goblins.

'Silence numskull! You were drunk. Wait 'til Maleaver hears about it. You will be lucky if you still live tomorrow.'

'Oh please my Lady, don't tell him.' A chorus of goblin voices joined in to plead with Silveria. She pushed them aside and opened the door of the carriage.

'Let's get going. We will be at the castle in a few hours. I will ride in the carriage to keep an eye on the prisoners, since you say they are so clever. Now get running.'

The goblins began to complain again that they were tired, however, they had no choice but to jog as the unicorns set off at a trot.

Inside the carriage there was much discussion in hushed voices. The friends talked about what they would do when they reached the castle. Lucy's stomach was feeling very queasy and she didn't think it was just travel sickness. Ellie wondered if Karate could really help in the fight against powerful magic. Perizam and Silveria knew that they were no match for Maleaver. As they were talking, Gabriella began to come round. The others watched, nervously. Gabriella sat up, slowly and focused on Silveria who was sitting next to her.

'How are you Princess?' asked the dryad.

Gabriella smiled. 'All the better for seeing that you are restored.' The fairy and the dryad hugged each other.

'How do you feel?' asked Lucy.

'A little shaky but I'll be fine,' Gabriella said.

They told Gabriella what they had been discussing and continued to make plans. It wasn't long before the carriage came to a halt.

'We are at the gates,' said Silveria, looking out of the window. 'I must play my part.'

'Play it well,' said Perizam. 'Much rests on them believing that you are still under enchantment.'

Chapter Thirteen

Maleaver's Castle

'Silveria took a deep breath and put her head out of the window.

'Open the gates,' she demanded of the gatekeeper. 'I have the Lord Maleaver's prisoners.'

The gatekeeper opened the gates at once, bowing as Silveria and the goblins passed through. The carriage clattered into the courtyard and came to a halt. Silveria got out. She turned to the unicorns and whispered, 'Thank you my friends. Soon you will be free.'

The unicorns gave a slight nod of their beautiful white heads and a shake of their silvery manes. At once, several guards and stable hands approached the carriage. The guards were not at all like people, more like large pigs with tusks, standing on their hind legs. They were dressed in red uniforms, which made them look rather ridiculous as well as frightening.

'These prisoners of are of greatest importance to my Lord Maleaver. I wish to see to it myself that they are locked securely in the dungeons along with the other fairy prisoners.'

'Very well my Lady,' said the chief guard. 'Come with us.' Then he turned to the other guards. 'Get the prisoners out.'

The guards grabbed Lucy, Ellie, Gabriella and Perizam and pulled them from the carriage. These strange creatures had hands, of sorts, with a thumb and two fingers. Gabriella stumbled and fell to the ground, still feeling weak. A guard roughly dragged her to her feet.

'Hey, be careful!' said Ellie.

'Quiet!' the guard snapped, shoving Ellie forward so that she too stumbled.

'Careful with them,' said Silveria. 'Remember their importance. They are not to be harmed. Lord Maleaver wants to make examples of them when he is crowned King of Elysia. He doesn't want useless slaves.'

The guard muttered something and the party made their way across the courtyard towards the entrance to the dungeons. Silveria knew she had only a short time to use her magic before they reached the dungeon. Once inside Maleaver had set up a powerful force field to prevent magic being used. Silveria walked behind the others. She could see three fat keys dangling from each of the guards' belts. She looked around her to make sure no one else was watching, then she pointed a finger at one bunch of keys. They lifted, as silently as a feather, from the man's belt and floated into Silveria's hand. She slid them into a pocket in her dress. She hoped that it would not be this guard who was going to unlock the dungeons.

They reached the door and the guard at the front unlocked it. Immediately inside was a flight of narrow steps leading down into a dark passage. There was a little light from small burning torches attached at intervals along the walls. Lucy tried to reach for Ellie's hand but a guard stood in between them.

'Have courage little one,' Perizam whispered from behind her. For that he received a swipe from his guard.

They walked through a maze of corridors and Ellie wondered how they would ever find their way back out. For Gabriella, there was an excitement, despite the fear, because soon she would see her parents again. The corridors eventually opened up into a huge cavern. Around the edge of it there were smaller caves carved out of the rock. Across their entrances were bars, making the caves into cages. As they entered the cavern two people rushed to the front of their cave and peered through the bars. One of them gave a gasp.

'Gabriella!' she cried.

'Mother!' Gabriella tried to run to her mother, but the guard beside her held onto her. 'Let me go!'

'Let her go, you thug,' said the man next to the queen.

'Father!' cried Gabriella.

'Be quiet, prisoner,' the guard growled. 'Put them in here' he said, leading the party to another cave.

'Put Gabriella with her parents,' said Ellie.

'You don't give the orders, you little whelp,' said
the guard. He opened the cage door and the prisoners
were bundled inside. Ellie kicked her guard as she was
being pushed into the cage.

'Ow! Why you little…' he hauled Ellie back out of
the cage. 'I shall have to teach you a lesson.'

Silveria saw this confusion as her one chance.
Quickly, she slipped the keys to Perizam, who was
waiting for them. He hid them in his cloak. The guard
had raised his fist over Ellie.

'Enough!' shouted Silveria. 'Put her in with the
rest. She will be taught a lesson, but that is for Lord
Maleaver to do, not you.' The prisoners were locked
inside the cage. 'Now go and round up those good
for nothing goblins and teach *them* a lesson for their
drunkenness that nearly lost us these prisoners.'

The thought of giving the goblins a good hiding pleased the guards. They began to laugh and talk about what they would do. 'Now I must go to Lord Maleaver. He will be expecting me.'

As the guards and Silveria departed, she looked back and smiled hopefully at her friends. This did not go unnoticed by Queen Hermia and Prince Lysander.

'Is she...'

'Yes father, she is on our side. Look.' Gabriella held out her hand to Perizam and he gave her the bunch of keys. She held them up so that her parents could see them.

'Oh darling we thought we'd never see you again. We thought...' The queen began to sob.

'Don't cry, Mother. These are my friends. Grizzle thought he'd got rid of me to the human world but Ellie found me. She didn't even believe in fairies until we met.'

'Yes, sorry about that,' said Ellie.

'But she saved me and her friend Lucy found out how to get us back here. Then we met Perizam...'

'It is so good to see you old friend,' said Prince Lysander. 'You must have been a great help to Gabriella.

Perizam only bowed his head.

'Oh yes Father, without him we could not have found you.'

'And now, we need to get out of here,' said Lysander. Gabriella slipped her hand through the bars and turned the key in the lock. The door opened. She rushed across to her mother and father, unlocked their door and flung herself into their arms. There were a few moments when no one said anything.

Then Perizam spoke. 'Come, we must leave but there are guards at the top of the stairs.'

'Can you help us find the way out of these tunnels?' asked Lucy.

'I will try,' said Perizam.

'What about the guards?' said Lucy.

'We'll tackle them,' said Ellie. 'Don't forget Karate Lucy.'

Lucy grinned, remembering Nikki Walters on the toilet floor.

Lysander laughed. 'This girl has spirit. I'd like to see this Karate thing, Ellie.'

Perizam had a very good sense of which way to go. He never once took a wrong turn and it wasn't long before the steps loomed up in front of them.

'Outside, at the door are two guards,' said Perizam.

'Will that door be locked?' asked Ellie.

'I should think so,' said Queen Hermia.

'The door opened outwards, I noticed,' said Lucy. 'If we could unlock it quietly we could use it to knock at least one of them out of the way.'

'Good idea, Lucy,' said Lysander.

There was a small arched window in the door with bars across it. Lysander reached the top of the stairs first and carefully peered out. He could see one guard pacing back and forth across the door while the other was picking at his hoof with a stick and grunting.

'Gabriella, bring the keys,' he whispered.

She squeezed past the others on the stairs. 'When we are out we must make our way to the stables. The unicorns will be waiting for us with the carriage.'

'But what about Silveria? We can't leave her,' said the queen.

'She said if she was not waiting for us it meant she could not get away and we must leave,' said Gabiriella.

'We must, my dear,' Lysander added. 'We have to get back to Elysia, set the fairies free from the enchantment and rally the forces against Maleaver.'

'Silveria is very brave,' said Queen Hermia.

'Right, on my count Gabriella, fling open the door. Ellie and I will take out these two oafs.' Lysander winked at Ellie. She felt proud that he thought her up to it. Silently, Gabriella turned the key in the lock. As the guard turned to come back across the door, Lysander counted. 'Three, two, one, NOW!'

Gabriella flung open the door, knocking the guard flying. The noise alerted the other guard. He jumped up and lowered his tusks to charge. Ellie was ready for him and easily brought the great hulk to the floor. He was stunned for a moment and Perizam, Gabriella and Lucy pounced on him. Before he had time to get up they had flung him down the steps and locked the door. Meanwhile, Lysander was taking on the other guard, who had managed to get up from being knocked over by the door. Lysander was quick and nimble. He dodged round the back of the big bulky guard, grabbing his arms, and with a mighty heave, thrust him towards the door. Gabriella opened it just in time and he joined his friend, who was groaning at the bottom of the steps. Gabriella locked the door.

Standing in the deserted courtyard, they half expected to see other guards come running out towards them, but no one came.

'We've done it,' Lucy whispered.

'Not quite. Now to find the stables. Keep to the wall in single file. Someone may be looking out of a window,' said Lysander.

'When we arrived I watched which way they led the unicorns: It was in that direction,' said Lucy, pointing across the courtyard to an archway.

'Smart girl,' said Queen Hermia. 'My Gabriella has made two great friends.'

'Come on then,' said Ellie. 'Let's get out of here before they spot us.'

Lysander led the way. They crept quietly, keeping to the walls and ducking under windows, constantly on the watch for doors opening. One opened, almost as they were upon it. They tried to melt into the wall. Fortunately the door opened between them and the person coming out so they were shielded by it. The kitchen boy, carrying dishes, was not aware of them. He didn't even close the door. When he had disappeared into another door, they hurried on. They reached the archway and went through it. Lysander peered round the corner.

'There are two people in the stable,' said Perizam.

'Probably stable hands,' said Gabriella.

'Maybe it's Silveria,' said Ellie.

'She would be on her own,' said Gabriella.

'I think it may be time to use some magic,' Queen Hermia suggested. She stepped forward and into the stable. Two boys looked up from raking hay. They looked confused. 'Sorry about this,' said the queen. She lifted her hands and froze them. 'It will wear off in an hour or so,' she said, patting one on the head.

The others appeared at the door. The unicorns were at the far end of the stable and the carriage was just outside. 'No sign of Silveria,' said Gabriella in dismay. 'I really don't want to leave her here. She is in great danger.'

'If she isn't here by the time we have the unicorns hitched up to the carriage, we must go,' said Lysander.

He and Queen Hermia went to talk to the unicorns. The unicorns trotted willingly to the carriage once more to help the queen and prince. They were all helping with the carriage when Lucy spotted her.

'Silveria!' she cried and ran towards her. 'You made it.'

The others looked up and Ellie and Gabriella ran to her too. As they reached her, they saw she was crying.

'What's wrong?' asked Gabriella.

'I'm so sorry,' she sobbed.

At that moment guards began to stream towards them from every opening. They were surrounded.

Ellie backed away from Silveria in horror. 'You betrayed us again!'

'No, no, it was Maleaver. He guessed I was no longer under his spell. He didn't take long to work it out. He insisted on seeing the prisoners and when I tried to stall him, he knew. He decided to use me to find you. He is going to turn me into a hob goblin slave with the rest of you.'

The guards grabbed each of them. 'Lord Maleaver wants to see you,' sneered the chief guard.

The party was pushed and pulled into the castle, along corridors, until they reached two large, grand doors.

'The throne room,' gasped Queen Hermia.

The room was not large, as the doors had suggested, but very grand. At one end was a throne and on it was seated Maleaver. Ellie had expected him to be an ugly goblin. Lucy had expected a hideous monster. Instead, they saw a handsome fairy-man, like Lysander, only broader and taller. He stood up. His face, although handsome, was twisted with rage.

'So ... the traitor,' (he glared at Silveria) 'the prisoners, the rescuers and the ...' he looked at Ellie and Lucy for a moment, 'human children, how sweet.'

He walked towards them and ran his finger round their faces. Ellie jerked away and Lucy cowered into Queen Hermia.

'And the lost princess has been found. Well, now I have a full set.'

'Let the human children go,' said Perizam. 'They are of no value to you. Send them back to their world; they can do no damage to you there.'

'Be quiet you woodland worm,' snapped Maleaver. 'They got here in the first place and look how far they've come. No, they will also be my slaves.'

Lucy could be brave no longer and began to cry. Ellie reached for her hand.

'Let's start with you shall we?' Maleaver walked towards Silveria. 'You have shown where your loyalties lie: With the fairies. Therefore I have no further use for you. Pity.' He touched her cheek, gently. Then he pushed her away from him. She stumbled. Suddenly she was gone and in her place was a silver birch tree. Everyone gasped.

'You can't do that!' protested Gabriella.

'I just did, didn't I?' Maleaver said. 'You can be next if you like, Princess. I shall turn you and your friends into, now let me see, ah yes, little ornaments of yourselves. Then you can't cause me anymore trouble before I become ruler of Elysia.'

He raised his hand towards Gabriella. As he did so, Ellie flung herself in front of the princess.

'No!' she shouted.

The magic hit her but instead of turning into an ornament she remained the same. Maleaver was confused and so was everyone else. Suddenly, Lucy felt incredibly angry. She flung herself at Maleaver's legs.

He was unprepared for this show of bravery and lost his balance. In a flash Ellie too was holding him down. Queen Hermia and Prince Lysander rushed forward and hit Maleaver with a bolt of their own magic. He was instantly turned into a mouse.

'That should keep him out of trouble for a while,' smiled the queen. The mouse scuttled away to a dark corner. She turned to Silveria and touched her forehead. The tree was transformed back into the dryad.

'Come on,' said Perizam, 'We must go. There are guards outside the room. The unicorns are waiting for us.'

They burst out of the throne room, taking the guards by surprise. Queen Hermia and Lysander used their magic to pin the guards to the wall. The friends hurried towards the stables once more.

'Stop!' shouted a goblin voice behind them. Ellie looked round. It was Grizzle and he had several goblins and guards with him.

'Hurry!' Ellie urged. They climbed quickly into the carriage and it sped towards the gate. The gatekeeper saw them coming and rushed to close the gate. The unicorns slowed down as the gates began to close. Grizzle and his band were coming up from behind. Gabriella leaned out of the window and with all her magical strength she held the gates open. The unicorns gathered speed again and the carriage hurtled through the gates. Then Gabriella turned and pulled them shut, locking them with the most powerful magic she could muster. At that she fell back, into an exhausted faint.

'Gabriella!' the queen cried, holding her limp body.

'She has not yet recovered all her magical power your majesty,' said Perizam. 'Whenever she uses any magic this happens.'

'It has been getting worse,' said Lucy.

'We must get her back to Elysia and underneath some fairy moonlight,' said Prince Lysander.

The journey seemed long. They were all tired and slept as much as they could. At dawn the next day they arrived at a most beautiful castle. Even in the hazy light Ellie and Lucy could see the sandy coloured towers, standing like guards on duty and the gardens filled with flowers.

Gabriella had still not woken up and the queen was very worried about her.

They got out of the carriage in the castle courtyard. It felt rather eerie.

'Where is everyone?' asked Lucy.

'The fairies are still under the enchantment, which makes them dull. They can't be bothered to do anything, so they're probably still in bed,' said Prince Lysander.

'We shall soon put it right though,' said Queen Hermia. 'Perizam, can you remember the way to the guest rooms?' Perizam nodded. 'Take our guests and find some food for yourselves. We will take Gabriella with us. We need to work some powerful magic of our own to remove the enchantments on our people and to restore the sun and moon to our land.'

Perizam led the way to the guestrooms. They were magnificent rooms with four poster beds and lavish furniture. Ellie and Lucy were put in one room and Perizam led Silveria to another, promising to bring food back with him.

Ellie threw herself on a bed. 'Mmm … this is sooo comfortable. Way better than my bed at home.'

Lucy bounced up and down beside her. 'It's great isn't it? Things will be all right now, won't they?'

Ellie nodded and they both began to bounce and giggle until they fell into a jiggling heap.

Chapter Fourteen

Restoring Elysia

Perizam returned with food and they tucked in to it hungrily.

'Look,' he said, pointing out of the window. The girls turned to see the room filling with warm, golden light. They rushed to look out. The sun was shining brightly, making everything sparkle again. The colours of the flowers stood out, the grass was bright green. The lake, down below in the garden, sparkled, reflecting a perfect blue sky. Then they saw fairies begin to come out of houses and rise up to fly. There was a buzz of excited voices as the fairies realised that they were back to normal. Many headed towards the castle to see if they could see the Queen and Prince. Some called out,' Queen Hermia! Prince Lysander! You are safe. Hooray!'

'Come on, we've got to find the Queen and Prince,' said Ellie. Silveria appeared at their door.

'How wonderful to see Elysia restored,' she said.

The friends left their rooms in search of the royal family. Servant fairies came from different rooms in the castle to greet them.

'The Queen and Prince are in their private rooms,' said one fairy, in a shimmering royal uniform. 'They are expecting you.'

'Come in,' said Queen Hermia. She greeted them all with a kiss to both cheeks. 'Elysia is free again. And we have you to thank; all of you.'

Everyone was embarrassed and protested that everyone else was the most important.

'But where is Gabriella?' asked Ellie.

'She is still asleep,' said the Queen, 'but tonight the moonlight will make her fully well again. Now that power has been returned to its rightful place, the moon will shine and Gabriella will feel its power over her. We will have a party.'

Soon Elysia was a hive of activity. The grounds of the castle were decorated in fairy lights and lanterns. A huge banquet was prepared and musician fairies brought their instruments to form an orchestra. As it began to get dark the fairies gathered. Queen Hermia and Prince Lysander came out of the castle to the sound of applause. In his arms the prince carried Gabriella and laid her on large cushions on the grass. A hush fell over the fairies.

The Queen made a speech. 'My dear fairies, nymphs, dryads and all who have been able to join us tonight, we are so pleased to be back with you. Our beautiful land is restored and we will take measures to protect it even more than before. Our daughter, Princess Gabriella is sick from her ordeal, but tonight the moon will bring about her recovery. Our friends Perizam, Silveria, Ellie and Lucy have risked all to save our land from destruction by the evil Maleaver. Tonight our party is in their honour.'

The four stepped forward and a loud cheer went up. 'Let us eat, drink and dance!' said Prince Lysander.

The musicians played and the fairies and their friends began to dance and eat. Ellie and Lucy had a wonderful time sampling fairy food and dancing to the enchanting music. The moon shone brightly over the whole kingdom, but it shone a special concentrated beam on Gabriella. As fairies came to look at her, she was lit, as if in a spotlight. Queen Hermia never left her side. Finally she began to stir. She yawned and stretched as if waking from the most restful sleep. She smiled up at her mother.

'Hello my darling,' said Queen Hermia. 'How do you feel?'

'Magical,' Gabriella replied.

Lucy and Ellie heard the news that she was awake and came running to meet her. The three friends hugged each other tightly.

'Soon we will have to leave,' Ellie said.

'I know,' said Gabriella. 'I'm glad we met. You will always be my friends. I will come and visit from time to time.'

Lucy's eyes lit up. Even Ellie was pleased, now that she believed in fairies.

The next morning Queen Hermia, Prince Lysander and Gabriella gathered to say goodbye to Ellie and Lucy. Perizam and Silveria were to escort them to the wood where they had arrived in Fairyland, so that they could find the same path back to the human world.

'Thank you Perizam and Silveria. You have been faithful friends.'

Perizam nodded and Silveria curtsied.

'We will miss you,' said Lucy.

'And we will miss you,' said the queen. 'We will never forget you and all that you have done for us. You are brave Lucy.'

'And Ellie, you will never doubt that fairies exist again,' said Gabriella, squeezing Ellie's hands.

They all hugged each other.

When they reached the wood they said a sad goodbye to Silveria and Perizam.

'We won't forget you,' said Ellie.

'Always remember how brave you have been here,' said Perizam. 'You will need it in your world too.'

'Goodbye, and take care,' said Silveria. 'The dryads will hear of your courage.'

Lucy and Ellie waved, and as they walked down the path Perizam and Silveria saw them disappear. Ellie and Lucy held tight to each other as they were pulled back into their own world. They landed by the woodpile and found themselves to be back to normal size. All was quiet in the garden. The girls headed back to the house, wondering how long they had been away and if search parties had been sent out for them.

Callum met them in the kitchen. 'Where have you been? Why didn't you come and find me? I waited ages.'

The girls looked at each other. 'Sorry Cal,' said Ellie. 'Where were you? I gave up looking.'

'I was in the shed, Lucy knew. She told me to hide there.'

'Oh but I couldn't give you away,' said Lucy.

'Well I'm not playing with you two ever again,' said Callum, storming off.

'That's a relief!' said Ellie. 'We mustn't have been away long in our time.'

Just then Ellie's mum came into the kitchen. 'Hi you two. You've been tucked away somewhere haven't you? Callum has looked everywhere for you. You ready for tea? What have you been up to?'

'Tea sounds great Mum,' said Ellie. She glanced at Lucy. 'We've been down the garden ... erm ... just doing stuff.'

Ellie's Mum gave her a suspicious look.

'We've been playing fairies,' said Lucy.

Ellie's Mum laughed out loud. Ellie looked embarrassed.

'Well, Lucy may make a girl out of you yet,' said her Mum.

They had tea and soon it was time for Lucy to go home.

'See you at school on Monday,' Lucy said.

'Yeah, said Ellie. Then hesitantly she said, 'Lucy, don't go telling people about what happened, they'd think we were crazy.'

Lucy smiled. 'I know. And you've still got your reputation to think about, even if you do believe in fairies now.'

Ellie smiled. 'Thanks. I wonder if we'll ever see Gabriella again. I hope so.'

'Me too.'

'You know, I keep wondering why Maleaver's magic didn't work on me.'

'Oh that's easy,' said Lucy. 'I read that in a book about fairies. Human bravery, where the person is willing to risk all, can be powerful against evil fairy